7496 9188

Disney

# Finding Tinker Bell

## a Never Girls adventure

# up the misty peak

written by Kiki Thorpe

illustrated by Jana Christy

A STEPPING STONE BOOK™

WITHDRAWN

Random House 🏠 New York

*For Eleanor —K.T.*
*For Tammy —J.C.*

*Library of Congress Cataloging-in-Publication Data*
Names: Thorpe, Kiki, author. | Christy, Jana, illustrator.
Title: Up the Misty Peak / written by Kiki Thorpe ; illustrated by Jana Christy.
Description: New York : Random House, [2019] | Series: Disney Finding Tinker Bell,
a Never Girls adventure ; 4 | A Stepping Stone Book.
Identifiers: LCCN 2018056332 | ISBN 978-0-7364-3873-5 (paperback) |
ISBN 978-0-7364-3874-2 (lib. bdg.) | ISBN 978-0-7364-3883-4 (ebook)
Subjects: | BISAC: JUVENILE FICTION / Media Tie-In. | JUVENILE FICTION /
Fantasy & Magic. | JUVENILE FICTION / Social Issues / Friendship.
Classification: LCC PZ7.T3974 Up 2019 | DDC [Fic]—dc23
rhcbooks.com

Printed in the United States of America

10 9 8 7 6 5 4 3 2 1

This book has been officially leveled by using the F&P Text Level Gradient™ Leveling System.

# Never Land...
# and Beyond

Far away from the world we know, on the distant Sea of Dreams, lies an island called Never Land. It is a place full of magic, where mermaids sing, fairies play, and children never grow up. Adventures happen every day, and anything is possible.

Though many children have heard of Never Land, only a special few ever find it. The secret, they know, lies not in a set of directions but deep within their hearts, for believing in magic can make extraordinary things happen. It can open doorways you never even knew were there.

One day, through an accident of magic, four special girls found a portal to Never Land right in their own backyard. The enchanted island became the girls' secret playground, one they visited every chance they got. With the fairies of Pixie Hollow as their friends and guides, they made many magical discoveries.

But Never Land isn't the only island on the Sea of Dreams. When a special friend goes missing, the girls set out across the sea to find her. Beyond the shores of Never Land, they encounter places far stranger than they ever could have imagined. . . .

This is their story.

# Shadow Island

# chapter 1

On a dark, moonless night, four fairies sat around a small campfire. The fire was not much bigger than a candle flame, and the fairies huddled close to it.

Normally, the fairies' own golden glows would have brightened the night. But their glows were now faint. The flames provided the only light, which flickered across their worried faces.

Shadows, cast by the fire, played across a rock behind them. If the fairies had been paying attention, they would have noticed something strange. Although there were four of them, five shadows conferred on the rock. One in particular seemed alert. It tilted its pert head toward the campfire, as if trying to hear better.

But the fairies didn't notice. They were deep in conversation.

"What can it mean?" the garden-talent fairy Rosetta whispered. She wore a leaf around her shoulders like a shawl to keep warm. As she spoke, she pulled it tighter. "Why would Tink write her name on this rock?"

"It's a message," the light-talent fairy Iridessa replied. "The question is, who is it for?"

"Maybe it's for the sprites in the Dark Forest," the animal-talent fairy Fawn said.

"They found her shoe, after all. Maybe she was trying to get it back." She patted the small leaf-satchel that held Tink's pom-pom slipper. The sprites had given it to them in exchange for their help bringing light to their village.

"But the sprites never met Tink," Rosetta pointed out. "Besides, they never leave the forest. Why would she leave them a message here?"

"Maybe it's a message to herself," said Silvermist, who sat back from the fire. She was a water-talent fairy and didn't like flames. "The rock is near the Lost Coast. Tink might have put it there in case she got lost so she could find her way back."

"But if Tink was on the Lost Coast, wouldn't we have found her?" Iridessa asked. "We searched up and down that beach. We didn't see any trace of Tink or her boat."

"That's not true." Silvermist leaned forward, lowering her voice. "Don't forget what I saw there in the fog. It looked like Tink, but it wasn't. It was like . . . the *ghost* of Tink." She shivered.

The other fairies shivered, too, except Iridessa, who frowned.

"Stop that," she scolded Silvermist.

The water fairy's eyes widened. "What?"

"Don't scare everyone with silly superstitions," Iridessa said. "I don't know what you saw. But I'm sure Tink is alive and well, somewhere on Shadow Island."

Iridessa gathered a ball of firelight, squeezing it thoughtfully as if it were putty. Golden light shone between her fingers.

"You know what I think?" she said at last. She released the ball of light. It hung in the air, then faded. "I think she wrote that message for *us*. Tink wants someone to know she's here. She needs help."

"That may be," Rosetta said. "But we can't assume anything. From now on, we have to make choices carefully. We have only the fairy dust left on our wings. When it's gone, our magic will be gone, too."

"Rosetta's right," Iridessa said. "It's going to be harder from here on. Anyone who wants to quit, speak up now."

The fairies looked at one another across the fire.

"Not me," said Fawn.

"Me either," said Silvermist.

"I'm here until we find her," said Rosetta.

Iridessa nodded. That settled it.

"But what about the girls?" Silvermist asked.

They all turned to look at the four human girls—Kate McCrady, Lainey Winters, and Mia and Gabby Vasquez— asleep nearby. To the tiny fairies, their slumbering forms were like small mountain ranges.

As they watched, the smallest girl, Gabby, turned over in her sleep and sighed. The fairies sighed, too.

"When our magic is gone, we won't be able to take care of them," Iridessa said. "They ought to be at home with their families. They're only children, after all."

"If we knew the way to Never Land, we could send them back to Pixie Hollow," Rosetta said. "From there they could find their way home."

The other fairies nodded in agreement. Whatever happened, they needed to make sure the girls got home safely.

"We should sleep," Iridessa said. "Silvermist, will you put out the fire?"

"Gladly," replied the water fairy. She plucked a few dewdrops, cradling them in her arms. When her arms were full, she threw the droplets on the fire. The flame sizzled out.

Silvermist sighed. "I'll miss doing that when my magic's gone. Fawn, what is it?"

The animal fairy was staring at the side of the rock.

"I thought I saw—" She shook her head. "Never mind. My eyes were playing tricks on me. Let's get some sleep."

*

Lainey lay awake in the darkness long after the fairies had gone to sleep. She had heard everything they said.

Lainey, her friends, and the fairies had been on Shadow Island for days,

searching for Tinker Bell. Lainey had never doubted that they'd find her. She believed in the fairies with all her heart. If they worked together, they could do anything.

But now she realized the fairies didn't see it that way. Lainey and her friends were a burden! Iridessa's words echoed in Lainey's mind. *When our magic is gone, we won't be able to take care of them.*

Lainey sighed. The fairies were in trouble. If only there was something she could do to help them in return. But she had no magic. No special talents. What could she do?

She turned onto her back. Without her glasses, the stars were only distant blurs. Lainey picked out a silvery smudge and made a wish. She wished for what she always wished for. She wished for magic.

But as she closed her eyes to sleep, Lainey knew that she'd made the wrong wish. This time, they needed more than magic.

They were going to need a miracle.

# chapter 2

Fawn knew that something was wrong as soon as she opened her eyes.

She uncurled from her wildflower, pushing back the petals she'd used as blankets. She stretched her wings, sat up, and looked around.

The girls lay asleep on the grass. The fairies were asleep, too. Fawn could see Rosetta's foot in its rose-petal slipper peeking out from a morning glory. The cold ashes from their small fire were scattered at the base of the rock.

Beyond the meadow where they'd camped, a lone mountain rose steeply. It made a dark shape against the blue predawn sky.

Everything was as it had been. Still, Fawn had the odd sense that a piece of the world was missing.

Nearby, something darted up from the grass. Fawn turned, startled. But it was only a moth. She watched it rise on silent wings.

Fawn knew then what had changed. Her magic was gone.

As an animal-talent fairy, Fawn had a certain kind of magic. It helped her communicate with beasts, birds, and bugs. But that wasn't all. Her magic was like a radio antenna picking up signals from the

animal world. She could read bees' moods
just by their buzzing. She sensed the
songbirds' sorrows and the worms' pride.
The pulse of animal life was like music
always playing in the background.

Now that music was gone. Fawn felt as
if she'd lost one of her senses.

Of course, she had known this would

happen as soon as she ran out of fairy dust. In Pixie Hollow, fairies got a teacup full of fairy dust every day. The dust wore off, little by little, until it was replenished. But Fawn had thought she'd have at least another day before hers was all gone.

"Well, I'll just have to make the best of it," she said aloud. She wasn't going to feel sorry for herself. Wallowing was for pigs.

Fawn flapped her wings. Fairies needed fairy dust to fly, too. But she still had wings. They ought to be useful for something.

Fawn fluttered hard. She rose into the air a few inches and turned in an awkward circle, like a flying beetle.

She landed and tried again. This time she pushed off hard with her feet. She sprang forward, flapping her wings, tracing a wide arc through the air.

"More like a grasshopper that time." Fawn smiled to herself. Now she was getting somewhere.

"Fawn?"

Fawn turned. Lainey was sitting up, watching her. "What are you doing?" Lainey asked.

"Just . . . getting some exercise." Fawn wasn't ready to tell her about the lost magic. Not yet.

Lainey studied Fawn. "You're not glowing."

Fawn glanced down. She noticed for the first time that her usual lemon-yellow glow had faded to a dull gleam.

That was another thing about fairy dust. It gave fairies their glow.

"Oh, that." Fawn rubbed her arm, as if that might make it shine again. "Hey, did you hear the one about the fairy who lost her glow?"

Lainey shook her head.

Fawn grinned. "She was a little dim."

Lainey didn't return the smile. Her thick glasses made her blue eyes look even bigger. With her wide-eyed, solemn expression, she reminded Fawn of a baby owl.

"Fawn, do you really think Tinker Bell is here?" Lainey asked.

"On Shadow Island?" Fawn nodded. "I do. And I still believe we'll find her."

"But why would she come *here*?" Lainey asked.

Fawn had wondered the same thing. What could have drawn Tink to this strange world, so far from Never Land? Had she been swept there by accident, pulled through the same mysterious portal that had brought them here? But then how could they explain the map of Shadow Island they'd found in Tink's workshop?

No, Fawn guessed Tink had come here for some purpose. "I suppose she came looking for something," she said to Lainey.

Lainey nodded. "I thought so. What do you think it was?"

Fawn shrugged. "We can only guess—"

She broke off as the sky suddenly grew darker. The air seemed to tremble.

Lainey glanced up. "What was that?"

A breeze swept through the meadow.

Fawn grabbed a blade of grass to keep from being blown away.

Lainey gasped and pointed into the wind. "Look!"

A great mass of clouds was coming toward them. It rolled and churned faster than Fawn had ever seen clouds move, tumbling with a force that seemed to come from within.

When the clouds neared the meadow, they cascaded toward the ground like a great frothing waterfall. The mist began to change shape. It became a herd of white horses. They galloped down the sky on silent hooves, trailing mist like smoke from a fire.

Lainey and Fawn stood frozen in place. They watched the sky creatures race toward them.

The herd touched down a short distance away. As they slowed, the breeze calmed. A heavy fog settled over everything.

Lainey turned to Fawn. Her big eyes shone with excitement.

"Oh, Fawn!" she whispered. "They're here. The mist horses!"

# chapter 3

Lainey had seen many magical things in her adventures with the fairies. But no sight was as heart-stopping as a herd of mist horses. The strange beasts were very rare. She had seen them only once before, on Never Land.

"What are they doing here?" she asked Fawn.

"They're not tied to any place. They travel the sky," Fawn said. "The wind must have blown them this way."

The silvery shapes of the herd were almost hidden in the mist.

"Come on, let's get a closer look!" Fawn started across the ground, fluttering forward in great hops.

Lainey glanced back at her friends. They were still asleep. The horses' silent arrival hadn't awakened them.

Kate lay closest to Lainey. Her red hair fanned out around her head. Her lips smiled gently, as if she was having a good dream.

Once, Kate had ridden a mist horse all the way across Never Land. No one knew how she'd tamed the magical creature. Kate had claimed they understood each other.

Lainey knelt down and gently touched Kate's shoulder. "Kate?" she whispered.

Kate rolled over. "No, *you're* a pizza," she murmured in her sleep.

Fawn was already several hops ahead. She paused and looked back. "Lainey?"

"Coming!" Leaving Kate there, Lainey hurried to catch up with Fawn.

As they went through the mist and saw the herd spread out before them, Lainey's breath caught. The horses' coats glistened with rain. Their long manes and tails were so pale and wispy it was hard to tell what was horse and what was vapor. They seemed to almost glow with an otherworldly light.

The horses were grazing. But as Lainey and Fawn approached, several lifted their heads. Lainey noticed that some of the mares had foals.

"Look, Fawn. Babies!" she whispered.

Fawn nodded. "We'll have to be careful. New mothers can be skittish. But he's the one to watch." She pointed to a huge horse with a coat like burnished steel. "That stallion is the leader."

They tiptoed closer. The horses flicked their ears forward and watched them. After a few moments, they seemed to decide Lainey and Fawn weren't a threat. They lowered their heads and returned to their meal.

At first, Lainey thought they were eating grass. But as she got closer, she noticed something. "They're only drinking the dew!"

"They're not like flesh-and-blood animals," Fawn reminded her. "They're born of the wind and rain. We can't expect them to act like normal creatures."

"Fawn, I just thought of something," Lainey said. "We saw these horses in Never Land, right? That must mean they know the way there."

Fawn looked at her. "Possibly."

"We could ride them back to Never Land!" Lainey said. "We can get more fairy dust, and then come back to find Tink!"

Lainey imagined riding the mist horses across the sky. A shiver of excitement ran down her spine. Was this the miracle she'd hoped for?

Fawn frowned. "What makes you think they'll let us ride them?"

"Kate did it," Lainey said. *And if Kate did it, so can I,* she added to herself. "Besides, we don't have any other ideas, do we? This might be our only chance."

Fawn nodded, considering the idea. "I'll try to talk to them. Maybe I can tell them what we need."

The fairy hopped closer to the nearest

horse. She let out a long whinny. Lainey thought she sounded just like a horse.

But the mist horse didn't even glance in her direction.

Fawn tried again. She snorted and whinnied. She tossed her head, letting her tiny braid whip like a mane.

This time the mist horse flicked an ear toward her. It raised its head and whinnied back.

"What did it say?" Lainey asked.

"I . . . I'm not sure," Fawn admitted.

Lainey was startled. Fawn could talk to any animal—feathered, finned, or furred. What did it mean that she couldn't talk to this one?

As they were talking, a little foal broke away from the herd and came closer. He stood with his knobby legs splayed wide, looking at them with bright curiosity.

Fawn chuckled. "Look at this bold fellow."

The foal had long silver eyelashes and a silky light-gray coat. His tail looked like a wisp of smoke. He raised his nose and snorted at them, as if to show how daring he was.

Lainey longed to reach out and pet the foal. But she didn't want to scare him. Better to let the foal come to her.

The brave little horse took a step toward her, then another. His mother, a large silver mare with a snow-white mane, watched closely. Not far away, the stallion was watching, too.

The foal was near enough to touch.

Lainey's heart pounded. Ever so slowly, she stretched out her hand.

The foal snorted at Lainey's fingers. Then, as if he had scared himself, he gave a little jump and danced away.

Lainey and Fawn laughed. The sound rang out in the silent meadow.

Suddenly, the stallion tensed. A second later, he spooked and bolted.

When they saw the stallion run, the other horses panicked. They charged after him.

Lainey gasped. They'd started a stampede!

A horse brushed past Lainey, knocking her down. She cowered on the ground. She was going to be trampled!

But the other horses passed right over her. They climbed into the air. Their hooves kicked up mist the way normal horses might stir dust.

Seconds later, they had sailed out of sight.

Lainey stayed huddled long after they were gone, waiting for her heart to slow. Gradually, the mist cleared. When she felt like she could breathe normally again, she stood up.

"Phew, that was crazy," she said. "Fawn, are you okay?"

There was no answer. Lainey looked around. A few small patches of mist were the only sign the mist horses had ever been there.

"Fawn?" Lainey called. "Fawn!"

Lainey heard a rustle behind her. She spun around.

Kate, Mia, and Gabby were walking toward her through the knee-deep grass. The other three fairies flew between them. The girls' faces were still puffy with sleep. Their hair was full of bits of grass.

Kate blinked in the morning light. "What did we miss?"

# chapter 4

Lainey sat on a rock in the meadow, trying to calm her shaking legs. Mia and Gabby sat on either side of her. Mia's arm was around Lainey's shoulders. Gabby kept patting her knee. The fairies hovered around her.

Only Kate stood apart. Her arms were crossed. She frowned as she watched them comfort Lainey.

"It's okay, Lainey," Iridessa said. "Just tell us what happened."

Lainey took a deep breath. "Fawn and I woke up early. We saw the mist horses land, so we went to get a closer look. But there was a stampede, and ..." The lump in her throat seemed to swell. "When the mist cleared, Fawn was gone."

"Just like the old myth," Silvermist whispered. "The one in the fairy books. The mist horses come and spirit their riders away."

"That's just a dumb old story," Kate huffed. "Cloud didn't carry *me* off, did she?" Cloud was the name Kate had given her mist horse.

Rosetta arched an eyebrow. "As I recall, she did."

"No one asked you, Rosetta," Kate said, glaring.

"Please don't argue!" Gabby cried.

"Gabby's right," Iridessa said. "We're all on edge. Everyone is worried about Fawn. But we need to keep our heads on straight and work together. That goes for you, too, Silvermist," she added, pointing a finger. "No more superstitious talk."

"Who's arguing?" Kate turned to Lainey. "I just don't understand why you didn't come get me. I *know* mist horses. I could have helped."

"I couldn't wake you up," Lainey murmured.

But she knew that wasn't exactly true. She'd barely tried. The truth was, she hadn't wanted Kate there. Kate was such a show-off. She would have bragged about the time she had tamed a mist horse and made it her friend. Maybe she would have tried to ride one again—and maybe the mist horses would have let her.

The worse part was, Kate didn't even *like* animals. At least, not as much as Lainey did.

And now look what had happened. Fawn was gone. And it was Lainey's fault.

Iridessa placed a tiny hand on Lainey's cheek. "Don't worry," she told Lainey. "There's nothing you could have done. Fawn knows animals, and she's as good a tracker as any scout fairy. She'll come flying back to us in no time."

"But . . ." Lainey wrung her hands. "Fawn can't fly."

Everyone stared at her.

"What do you mean?" Rosetta asked.

"She couldn't get up in the air this

morning. She was just hopping along the ground like . . . like a grasshopper," Lainey said.

The fairies exchanged looks.

"So, it's happened," Silvermist said. "I didn't think it would be so soon."

"What's happened? What are you talking about?" Mia asked.

"We're down to the fairy dust on our wings," Rosetta explained. "When it's all used up, our magic will be gone, too. It seems Fawn's magic was the first to go."

"This is even worse than I thought," Iridessa said. "We need to find her before she ends up in big trouble."

*Poor Fawn!* Lainey looked up at the sky. It was streaked with wispy clouds, like tracks the mist horses had left behind. If they followed them, they might find her. But how could they get all the way up to the sky?

Mia jumped to her feet. "Did you hear that?"

A soft snort had come from behind a nearby boulder.

"Something's there." Mia squeezed Lainey's arm. "And it's *spying* on us."

"Come on." Kate squared her jaw. "Whatever it is, we'll meet it together."

Holding one another's hands, the girls crept toward the rock. The fairies flew alongside them.

Just as they reached the boulder, they heard a high-pitched bleat. In a puff of mist, a spindly beast charged out from behind the rock.

Lainey gasped. It was the silver foal!

"A baby horse!" Gabby rushed forward, stretching out her arms as if to give him a hug.

But Lainey held her back. "Don't. You'll scare him."

The foal had stopped as soon as he saw them. He didn't look as bold as he had before. He shied away and let out another shrill whinny.

Lainey didn't speak Horse, but she could guess his meaning. *Help me,* he seemed to be saying. *I'm alone and scared.*

Lainey lowered her voice. She tried to sound like Fawn when she spoke to a frightened animal. "What are you doing here? Where's your mama?"

The foal eyed her through his long silver eyelashes.

"I don't see her anywhere nearby," Silvermist said. "I wonder if he got separated in the stampede."

"I'm sure his mother will be back to find him," Iridessa said.

"Maybe." Lainey didn't feel sure at all. The mist horses were long gone.

*If Fawn were here, what would she do?* Lainey asked herself. At once, she knew the answer. She would look after the foal. She would make sure he got back to his family.

She turned to her friends. "We have to find the herd. This baby needs his mama—and we need Fawn. Besides, the mist horses may know the way back to Never Land. If we can get them to take us there, we'll get the fairy dust we need." For once, she was going to help the fairies, rather than the other way around.

"But how will we reach them?" Mia asked. "We don't have enough fairy dust to fly."

Lainey's gaze traveled past Mia to the single mountain that rose above them. Clouds ringed its summit. The peak seemed to touch the sky.

"We can't fly," Lainey said. "But we can climb."

# chapter 5

High over Shadow Island, Fawn dangled
from a mist horse's tail. As the horse
galloped through the air, its tail swung
behind it, and Fawn swung with it. She
was getting dizzy, but she couldn't let go.
The ground was too far away.

Fawn had grabbed hold of the tail when
the herd had stampeded. She thought it
would be safer *on* a horse than under it.
But she hadn't counted on the horses

taking off. Before she knew it, she'd been carried into the sky.

The mist horse soared on, unaware of its fairy passenger.

How far were they going? Would they land again on Shadow Island? Or would she be spirited away to some unknown place?

If Fawn had had her magic, she could have let go and flown back to her friends. Without it, she was stuck like a burr.

The mist horse picked up speed. It seemed to be racing toward something, moving faster and faster. Fawn's eyes stung from the wind. The sky was just a blur.

Then, when it didn't seem the horse could go any faster—it vanished! One moment, it was there. The next, Fawn found herself clutching mist. The horse had simply evaporated.

Fawn scrambled in the air for a second. Then she fell.

Luckily, a fairy weighs no more than a handful of dandelion fluff. She didn't fall very fast.

Fawn spread her wings like a parachute. She glided down, down, down and landed with a bump that sent her head over heels.

"Beetles and bugs!" Fawn yelped as she rolled to a stop. She dusted herself off and looked around. She had landed on the side of a cliff.

Fawn sniffed the air. Now that her magic was gone, her other senses seemed sharper. She could see a ring of lichen a few feet below. She could hear water rushing somewhere far away. She could smell the fragile shoots of grass sprouting from crevices, and something else—the musky smell of a rodent.

The scent was strong. Fawn knew the animal was close by.

Maybe she could ask for help. But without her magic, would she be able to speak its language?

She spotted a hole in the ground almost hidden between two rocks. Fawn flutter-hopped over to it and sniffed again. Yes, it was definitely a rodent's home.

"Hellooooo?" Fawn called into the hole.

She heard scuffling, then silence.

"Knock, knock!" called Fawn.

No answer. Whoever was inside was clearly hoping she would go away.

"You're supposed to say 'Who's there?'" she hollered.

Fawn picked up a tiny pebble. She hefted it to the edge of the hole and dropped it in.

She heard a loud squeak. A moment later a pointed nose poked out of the hole. A beady-eyed rock rat came snuffling out.

The rock rat glared at Fawn. His long whiskers quivered indignantly. *Well?*

Fawn took a deep breath. She gave a long squeak in formal Rat that meant "Beloved brother, I am sorry to disturb you on this fine afternoon, but I am a traveler far from home—"

The rat cut her off. "Fine afternoon? Fine nothing!" he shrilled. "You must be a maniac to be out at this hour!"

Fawn gasped in delight. "You can understand me? I can understand you!"

She didn't need magic to talk to animals! Or maybe language was its own magic. Fawn was so happy, she danced around.

The rat stared at her as if she had

proved his point. "Stop that!" he snapped. "Are you insane? They'll see us."

"*Who* will see us?" Fawn asked.

"The hawk, of course!"

Fawn looked around. Far in the distance, a single hawk wheeled in the air. "Him? He's too far away to be any bother."

"He'll send his spy." The rat's eyes darted left and right. "This is no time of day to be out. No time at all."

*Spy?* Fawn was starting to think the rat was the crazy one. She decided to get to the point. "I've lost my friends. I need to get back to them, but I don't know where I am. Can you tell me?"

"You're at hole four hundred and forty-seven," said the rat. "It's right over the door, plain as day."

Fawn looked at the hole. She saw nothing there.

"Well, what's below us, then?" she asked.

The rat huffed. "Four-forty-six, I suppose."

"And above us?" Fawn asked.

"I really wouldn't know," said the rat. "Now, if you don't mind, I must be—" He broke off, his face twisted in fear. He was staring at something behind Fawn.

She turned. Nothing was there. Only a patch of darkness between the rocks.

"It's just a shadow," she said, turning back to the rat.

But he was already gone. She could see the tip of his tail disappearing down the hole.

Fawn was now sure that the rat was crazy. "Poor fellow. Running from shadows," she said to herself. She cupped her hands to her mouth and called down the hole. "Thanks any—"

The blow came out of nowhere, so hard that it knocked the wind out of her. For a second, Fawn thought the sky had fallen on her.

An instant later, she was pulled into the air, gripped in the hawk's sharp talons.

# chapter 6

"It's no use, Lainey," Mia said. "He just won't come."

Lainey pushed her glasses up. She studied the stubborn little mist horse. He stood with his long legs wide, eyeing her. The girls had tried and tried to catch the lost foal. But every time they got close, he darted away.

Gabby pulled up a handful of grass. She shook it at the foal. "Come on, horsey. Here's some yummy food for you."

The foal sniffed at the grass, then snorted.

"He doesn't eat grass," Lainey told Gabby. "He eats dew."

"Kate, you're the mist-horse expert," Mia said. "Can't you think of something?"

Kate snapped her fingers at the foal. "Come on. Let's go! Giddy-up!" She started to run, glancing back over her shoulder. "Follow me!"

The foal just blinked.

Kate shrugged and came back to stand with her friends. "He's not like my Cloud. She was a really *smart* horse." She chewed her lip. "If we had a lasso, we could pull him along."

"What could we use for a lasso?" Lainey asked. There wasn't a rope, or even a vine, in sight.

The fairies had been watching from a rock. Now Iridessa rose and fluttered over.

"We're going to have to leave him, Lainey," she said. "I'm sorry. I know you want to help. But we can't wait any longer or we may never find Fawn."

Lainey sighed. It broke her heart to leave the little lost horse behind.

Suddenly, she had an idea. "Iridessa, you're right! We have to leave him!"

Gabby gaped at her in dismay. "You're going to leave him? Just like that?"

"No, Gabby," Lainey whispered. "We're going to make him *think* we're leaving. Then maybe he'll follow us."

"Oh, like a trick!" Gabby said.

"That's right. A trick." Lainey took the younger girl's hand. "Come on, start walking, and don't look back. Pretend you don't even see him."

Lainey and Gabby started walking toward the mountain. Kate and Mia fell in behind. The fairies flew after them. No one even glanced at the foal.

Lainey counted one hundred paces. "Okay, Gabby," she said. "What's the foal doing now?"

Gabby peeked over her shoulder. "He's following us!"

Lainey grinned. Her plan was working! They had only needed to give the foal the choice to come.

The land began to rise. They had reached the base of the mountain. As they climbed, the foal got closer and closer. Soon he was walking just a few paces behind them.

"Can we name him?" Gabby asked.

Lainey thought about it. "He's not really ours to name. But just the same, we should call him something."

"We could call him Smokey," Kate suggested. "He's the color of smoke."

"Or Rain," Silvermist suggested. "Because he's as soft as a spring shower."

"Or Thistle," Rosetta said. "He reminds me of those silver flowers."

"Let's call him Andrew," said Gabby.

They all looked at her. "There's a boy at school named Andrew. He's nice," Gabby explained.

Lainey watched the foal trot. His hoofs kicked up puffs of mist as he ran. "I think we should call him Dewdrop. Because he's just a little thing the clouds left behind."

The foal raised his head. He flicked his ears forward.

"I think he likes that name," Mia said.

"Dewdrop it is," Kate agreed.

They walked on. The ground began to rise more steeply. Soon the girls were breathing hard. Lainey's throat ached with thirst.

But she was more worried about the foal. His head hung low. His silver coat looked dull and dry.

"We need to find some dew," Lainey said. "Or mist."

"Wait." Silvermist suddenly drew up short. Her head was cocked to one side, listening. "Do you hear that?"

Lainey heard a distant rushing. "Is it the wind?" she asked.

"No. Water! This way!" Silvermist darted ahead. The girls scrambled after her, clambering over the mossy, rocky mountain slope. As they came over a rise, they saw what made the sound.

A waterfall spilled down the mountainside. It ended in a clear, shallow pool. At the base of the falls, where the water splashed down, a cloud of mist rose into the air.

The girls ran to the edge of the pool. They fell on their knees and splashed the cool water on their faces.

Kate scooped up some to drink. She stopped with her hand halfway to her mouth. "Hold on. Is this safe?"

"Let me check," Silvermist said.

The water fairy plucked up a droplet of water. Holding it between her hands, she peered into it as if it were a crystal ball. She sniffed it. She stuck out her tongue and tasted it.

"Perfectly safe!" Silvermist declared.

The girls gulped handfuls of water. The fairies drank, too, dipping down like hummingbirds to skim water from the surface.

Dewdrop didn't want the water. He headed straight for the mist. He climbed into the pool and splashed across it to reach the cloud rising from the waterfall.

"Good idea, Dewdrop!" Kate said. She took off her shoes and jumped into the pool.

A minute later, all the girls had jumped in. They laughed and splashed one another.

Dewdrop whinnied and came toward them, lifting his knees high. He wanted to play, too!

Lainey splashed water on him. He darted away, then came back for more. As the mist and water collected on his coat, it began to shine. He looked like he had when Lainey first saw him in the meadow.

"Look, a rainbow!" Gabby said. The sunlight shining down on them made a faint, shimmering band of color in the mist.

"You call that a rainbow?" Iridessa scoffed.

Silvermist stood up. She and Iridessa

exchanged a grin. "*We'll* show you a rainbow."

The light and water fairies began to dart through the air above the pool. Their hands moved quickly, as if they were plucking invisible threads and weaving them together. As they moved back and forth, bands of color appeared in the air behind them—red, orange, yellow, green, blue. A brilliant streak of violet came last.

The fairies came to a stop. A beautiful rainbow arced over the pool. "Now, that's a rainbow!" Iridessa declared, dusting off her hands.

The girls clapped. "Fairies make the best rainbows," said Lainey.

"They're one of our specialties," Silvermist replied with a wink.

"Did fairies *invent* rainbows?" Gabby asked.

"Oh no," Silvermist told her. "One day, at the beginning of time, the sun looked down on Pixie Hollow. When she saw how beautiful it was, she cried tears of joy. That was how the first rainbow was made. Fairies have been copying them ever since."

Iridessa smiled and shook her head. "There you go with your myths again, Silvermist."

"Look at Dewdrop!" Mia exclaimed.

The foal had crossed the pool to reach the end of the rainbow. He raised one hoof and pawed the air, as if he was trying to climb onto it.

Gabby laughed. "He thinks it's a bridge!"

"Silly horse. You can't walk on a rainbow," Mia told Dewdrop.

Kate raised her eyebrows. "Who knows? Maybe where he comes from, you can."

Suddenly, they heard Rosetta cry out. She had been hovering beside the pool. But now she was sprawled on the ground.

Everyone rushed to her. "Rosetta, what's

wrong?" Silvermist asked, helping her up.

The garden fairy's face was pale. She flapped her wings hard, but she could only rise a few inches into the air. "My magic is gone," she whispered.

"Oh, Rosetta," Iridessa said, putting an arm around her shoulders. She and Silvermist exchanged worried looks. Two fairies had lost their magic. Who would be next?

*We have to find those horses,* Lainey thought. The mist horses were their only chance to get back to Never Land and get more fairy dust.

The girls silently climbed out of the pool. The joy had gone out of the afternoon, like a cloud crossing the sun.

"It's going to be a harder climb from

here," Kate said, looking up at the steep, rocky mountain.

Mia had stepped away to wring out her skirt. Suddenly, she called, "Hey, come look at this!"

A narrow trail led up the mountain-side. "That's where we go next," Mia said.

# chapter 7

High in the air, Fawn peered out from the
cage of the hawk's talons. One of her wings
was bent uncomfortably. But at least she
was in one piece.

Although Fawn couldn't see the bird's
head, she had a good view of its underside.
From its mottled feathers, she guessed it
was a goshawk.

Fawn felt a pinprick of hope. Goshawks
were one of the friendlier birds of prey.

Maybe she could talk her way out of this.

She cleared her throat. "Hello up there!" she squawked in Hawk.

The goshawk screamed in surprise. Clearly he hadn't been expecting his dinner to greet him. He paused, flapping his wings, and looked down to see exactly what he had picked up.

When he saw the fairy, his claws opened so fast Fawn had to grab onto a talon to keep from falling.

"I say!" the goshawk screeched. "Is that *Fawn*?"

Fawn was so busy trying to hold on that she hadn't taken a good look at the hawk's face. Now her mouth fell open in surprise. "Striker?"

Fawn had last seen Striker on Never

Land. She'd found him tangled in vine when he was only a hatchling. She had set him free and had never seen him again. She sometimes wondered what had happened to him.

"Yes! Yes, it's me!" the bird answered. "But what on earth are you doing here?"

"I could ask you the same. But, Striker, would you mind pulling me up? We're awfully high up here." Fawn wasn't sure she could hold on much longer.

"Of course." Striker flexed his claws, pulling Fawn back into their grip. He held her more gently now.

"This is awkward," the bird clucked. "We never would have snatched you up if we'd known it was you. From above, you looked like some sort of sparrow."

"It's all right," Fawn said. "But is there somewhere we can land? It's hard to talk like this."

"Of course. Our nest is just up ahead." Striker spread his wings and soared on.

Now that she wasn't worried about being a hawk's meal, Fawn paid more attention to the land flashing below. They were flying above a mountain. A great forest stretched out beyond it. Where were her friends now? Would she ever find her way back to them?

Striker sailed down toward a wooded area at the base of the mountain. He landed on the edge of a bowl-shaped nest. Carefully, he placed Fawn inside it.

The two faced each other. The goshawk's yellow eyes and the fierce

white stripes on his forehead made him look as if he were scowling. But he wasn't angry, only embarrassed.

"*Cuk-cuk-cuk,*" he chortled, ducking his head. "We truly are sorry for meeting you under these circumstances."

"Say no more, Striker. It was an honest mistake." Fawn wondered why he kept saying *we.* As far as she could see, they were the only two creatures in the nest. "I'm happy to see you again. You're all grown up. But what are you doing here? Why aren't you in Never Land?"

"Ah, now, that is an interesting story." Striker ruffled his wings and settled into the nest. "I was out flying one day in Never Land, when I was caught by a sudden storm. I sought shelter in a tree, but there were few to be found. I ended up in one that was no more than a bundle of sticks.

"The wind was fierce. I clung to my branch and barely managed not to blow away. My shadow, however, wasn't so lucky. The wind tore it clean off."

"Tore your *shadow* off?" Fawn asked, startled.

The goshawk nodded. "I saw it go

tumbling away. Of course, I chased it. Before I knew it, I'd been swept into the heart of the storm. And it spit me out here, on Shadow Island."

Fawn was struck by a sudden hope. "Do you think you could show me the way back to Never Land?"

"To be honest, I've never looked for it," Striker said. "We're happy here."

"Really?" Fawn looked around. "Striker, who is *we*?"

"My shadow and I," the bird replied.

"Shadow?" Fawn gaped at him.

"Don't tell me you didn't notice it there. It's the one that spotted you on the cliff."

Fawn suddenly remembered the shadow among the rocks, the one that had frightened the rock rat. "But that couldn't have been your shadow," she said. "You were too far away."

"We go our own ways now, my shadow and I," Striker explained. "Though we still keep an eye on each other. It's much easier to hunt with a loose shadow than one that's always following you around." He gave Fawn a sharp look. "I see yours is right on your heels. It must be quite attached to you to stay so close."

Fawn, who had not paid any attention to her shadow, now noticed something strange. Although she hadn't moved, her shadow was growing smaller and smaller. It appeared to be trying to squeeze up against her, the way a chick huddles under its mother's wing.

At the same moment, Fawn noticed

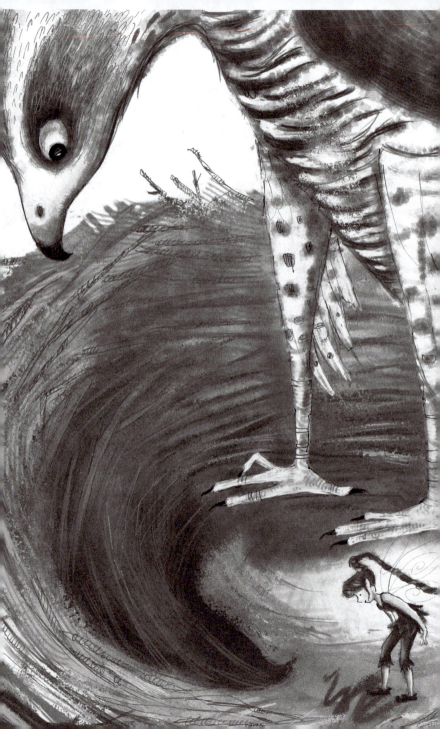

that Striker's shadow was leaning forward in a rather hungry way.

*"Mind your manners,"* Striker scolded his shadow. "Any friend's shadow is my friend, too."

His shadow straightened up. Of course, Fawn couldn't see its face. But she could tell by the way the shadow huffed and puffed that it was rather put out.

"You *talk* to your shadow?" she asked in amazement.

"Yes. And the best part is, it never talks back." Striker chuckled. "But enough about *us.* You haven't told me why you're here on Shadow Island."

"I'm looking for my friend Tinker Bell. She's missing." Fawn told Striker the story of how Tink had set out to sea in a toy boat and disappeared. "We have reason to believe she's here on Shadow Island," she explained.

"I haven't seen any fairies. I would have remembered that. But—" Striker narrowed his eyes. "You know, something you said rings a bell. Come with me." He turned to his shadow. "Stay here. We'll be back soon."

The shadow goshawk tossed its head, as if to say, *Fine. Suit yourself.*

Fawn climbed up on the edge of the nest. "Do you mind if I ride with you?" she asked. "I'm having a little trouble flying."

"Not at all," the bird replied. "Hop aboard."

Fawn fluttered up onto his back. She settled in the soft feathers between his wings. It was much better than riding in his claws. "Ready!" she called.

Striker spread his wings. As they lifted into the air, Fawn glanced back at the shadow goshawk. It perched on the edge of the nest like a ghostly guard.

Striker soared over the forest until they came to a beautiful waterfall. It spilled down the side of the mountain into a clear blue pool.

The goshawk flew down and landed on a ledge beside the waterfall.

"In there," he said as Fawn hopped down from his back. "Behind the water-fall. I'll wait here, if you don't mind. I don't like getting my wings wet."

Fawn flutter-hopped over to the waterfall. At first she couldn't see any way behind it. But after searching for a moment, she found a slippery ledge along the rock.

Spray from the waterfall dampened her wings and clothes as she shuffled along the ledge. A moment later, Fawn found herself in a shallow cave. The waterfall made a curtain on one side, shutting out much of the light.

As Fawn's eyes adjusted to the dimness, she spied a hulking shape in the darkness. Something was in the cave with her.

Her eyes traveled over a wooden hull, past a rope net, up to a little cabin. They came to rest on a golden bell.

She'd found Tinker Bell's boat!

# chapter 8

"Hello?" Fawn called. "Tinker Bell?" The rushing waterfall drowned out her voice.

Fawn flutter-hopped onto the deck. "Tink?" she called again.

The ship's bell hung from the side of the cabin. Fawn grasped the rope and pulled it. A golden note rang through the cave's gloom. The sound was so pretty and bright, it almost seemed as if Tink were there with her.

In the cabin, she found Tink's thistledown comforter and her favorite leaf-coat. Fawn picked up an empty acorn cup and sniffed it. It smelled faintly of chamomile tea. The room felt as if Tink had just left it and might return at any moment.

There was one more place to check. Fawn descended into the hold.

The boat's cargo area was musty and dank. Barrels filled the space. Fawn took the lid off one. It was half full of dried cherries.

*She brought food with her,* Fawn thought with surprise. From the look of it, Tink had meant to be gone for a long time.

Fawn picked a cherry and replaced the lid. When she bit into it, the sweet taste reminded her of Pixie Hollow. For a second, she was filled with longing for home.

The next barrel contained rainwater. Fawn took a long drink, wiping her mouth on her sleeve. She reached for the lid on the next barrel.

Fawn gaped in astonishment. She opened another barrel. Then another.

Fawn's hands trembled as she replaced the lids. Of all the things she'd thought she might find, she had not expected this. She knew she could not wait for Tink to return. She had to find her friends right away.

*

On the mountain, Lainey and her friends huddled together. The trail had led them up the mountainside, past rocks and over narrow streams, until they came to the edge of a dense wood.

The trees looked like ancient creatures. Their trunks were thick and knobby. Their branches twisted at strange angles.

"I don't like the look of this place,"

Rosetta said from her perch on Gabby's shoulder. She'd been riding there since they left the waterfall.

"That's what you always say. You said that about the Great Ones' forest," Iridessa reminded her. "And that turned out all right, didn't it?"

"I just hope *these* trees don't start talking to us," Mia said. "I'm not sure I'd like what they have to say."

"I don't see a way around," said Kate. "The faster we get through this forest, the sooner we'll be to the top."

They entered the woods, sticking close together on the path. Lower down, the trail wound back and forth across the mountainside. But here it rose steeply, as if whoever made it had wanted to get through the woods as quickly as possible.

Sunlight slanted down through the treetops, casting beams in the faint mist. Rather than making the forest brighter, they somehow enhanced the gloom.

Lainey shivered. "Did you hear something?" she asked her friends.

They stopped and listened. The silence was complete. No bird chirped. No breeze rustled the leaves. Yet Lainey was certain that something had disturbed the stillness.

Dewdrop stood tense and alert. His nostrils quivered.

"What is it, Dewdrop?" Lainey asked.

She tried to nudge him forward, but Dewdrop wouldn't move. His legs trembled. His eyes rolled, showing their whites.

Gabby gasped. "There's a wolf!"

They spun to look where she pointed. But it was only a shadow on the base of a tree trunk. It had the shape of a wolf's pointed ears and long snout.

Mia took Gabby's hand. "Don't worry. It's only a . . ."

She trailed off, her eyes going wide. The shadow was moving!

It slid across the tree trunk and vanished, then appeared again on the next tree. The shadow paused there, its jaw open. Its long tongue lolled out.

Something flickered in the corner of Lainey's vision. She looked up and saw the shadow of a bird alight on a branch. It hunched there, peering down at them. Deeper in the forest, she saw another dark shape scuttle across the ground and disappear into the undergrowth.

Fear squeezed Lainey's heart. What were these things? How could shadows move on their own?

A sudden blaze of light startled her. But it was only Iridessa flaring her glow. "Keep going," the light fairy told them. "They're only shadows. They can't hurt you."

Gabby eyed the wolf shadow. It had moved one tree closer. "Are you sure?"

Iridessa nodded. She was trembling with the effort of shining so brightly. "Don't let fear freeze you. Just stay calm and keep walking."

The girls did as she said. Lainey walked fast. Her fingers clutched Dewdrop's wispy mane to keep him beside her.

The wolf shadow followed them, moving from tree to tree. He seemed to want to come closer. But he stayed outside the ring of Iridessa's light.

Ahead, Lainey saw a break in the trees. Bright sunlight shone beyond them. They were almost out of the woods!

Lainey couldn't help herself. She broke into a run. As soon as he felt her move, Dewdrop bolted.

As if a dam had burst, Lainey's friends began to run, too. They spread out, abandoning the narrow trail.

A second later, they emerged into sunlight. Even though her lungs felt ready to explode, Lainey kept on running, until she was far, far away from the woods.

At last, the girls slowed. They stood gulping air and looked back at the trees.

The woods were still and silent. There was no sign of the shadows. If it hadn't been for her friends and Dewdrop panting next to her, Lainey would have thought she'd imagined them.

"Everyone okay?" Kate asked.

They all nodded. Dewdrop's thin legs were trembling. Lainey put a hand on his neck to try to calm him.

Rosetta climbed out of Gabby's pocket, where she'd hidden when they started to run, and asked, "Where's Iridessa?"

They found the light fairy just outside the woods. She was crouched on a patch of moss, where she'd fallen.

Kate gently picked up the exhausted fairy. "I'll carry you from here," she whispered.

No one asked Iridessa what had happened. They all knew.

The light fairy had used up the last of her magic.

# chapter 9

Lainey stood on a ledge, high up the mountainside. She twisted her fingers through Dewdrop's mane as she gazed upward.

They'd come to the end of the trail. Above her was a sheer rock face, too steep and slippery to climb.

"What's the matter?" Kate asked from behind. She tried to peer around to see why they had stopped.

"We can't go any farther," Lainey said. "There's no way up."

"Now what?" asked Mia.

Lainey didn't know. She had been so sure the herd of mist horses would be here when they got to the top of the mountain. Although a strong wind was blowing, there was no storm in sight. Fluffy white clouds dotted the bright blue sky like islands in a sea.

"Where's your mama?" Lainey whispered to Dewdrop.

The little horse whinnied, as if he was wondering the same thing.

Then, from high above, they heard an answering whinny!

A cloud in the near distance started to churn. The soft, wispy shapes at the

top darkened and became solid. The mist horses emerged from the cloud.

A great silver mare with a silky white mane came to the edge of the cloud and looked out at Lainey and her friends.

When Kate saw her, she gasped and pushed forward. "That's my Cloud! *Cloud!*" She waved her arms.

Lainey recognized her, too. "That's Dewdrop's mama!"

The mare whinnied. But she wasn't talking to Kate. She was calling to her baby. *Come here!*

Dewdrop answered her. *I can't!*

Cloud paced the edge of her cloud base. But she didn't come.

Dewdrop called more and more desperately. But the mare seemed unable to step off the cloud.

"He's crying! Why doesn't she come?" Gabby asked.

"I don't know," Lainey said. What was keeping the mare away?

In fact, the mare seemed to be moving farther from them. Lainey suddenly remembered what Fawn had told her in the meadow. *The wind must have blown them this way.*

"It's the wind!" Lainey said. "It's moving in the wrong direction. She can't fly against it."

Lainey nudged Dewdrop, trying to urge him toward his mother. The wind was in his favor. But he wouldn't budge.

"He wants to fly," Kate said. "But he's afraid to step off the cliff."

The cloud base with the herd was drifting farther away. How could they bridge the gap before it was gone?

Lainey suddenly recalled Dewdrop trying to climb the rainbow. She turned to Silvermist. She was the only fairy who could still fly.

"Could you make another rainbow?" Lainey asked. "One big enough to reach that cloud?" This time, Iridessa couldn't help—her magic was gone. But the sun was shining, and Silvermist still had magic left. Maybe it was enough.

"A rainbow can't hold him," Silvermist told her. "Not even a magic one."

"*I* know that," Lainey replied. "But *he* doesn't. Dewdrop can fly—he's a mist horse. We just need to help him believe that he can."

"I'll try." Silvermist rose into the air. She began to wind back and forth, like a spider spinning a web. Lainey knew that she was collecting threads of mist, trying to weave them into the rainbow's fabric.

A faint rainbow appeared. This one was

pale and watery, barely visible
against the sky.

Cloud had stopped
calling, but she hadn't
moved. She stood at the
edge of the cloud base,
looking out at them as the
wind pushed her away.

The rainbow only reached halfway to
the cloud when Silvermist fluttered back
to them. She fell to the ground, exhausted.
"I can't do anymore," she said. Her glow
had faded out.

Tears filled Lainey's eyes. They'd come
all this way. They were so close!

A hot tear rolled down her cheek. It
landed on the ground at her feet.

As Lainey stared at it, a dot appeared

next to it. Then another. Lainey looked up. Drops splashed against her cheeks. "Rain!" she cried.

"Where is it coming from?" Mia gazed up in wonder. There was no cloud above them. The sun still shone brightly, yet rain was falling.

"The sun is crying for us," Silvermist said. "Just like in the myth."

This time, Iridessa didn't correct her.

As the sun shone through the rain, a beautiful rainbow appeared. It stretched across the chasm to the cloud where Dewdrop's mother stood.

Lainey whispered in Dewdrop's ear. "There's your bridge, little guy. Go on. Go home to your mother."

Dewdrop took a tentative step off the

cliff and into the air. He scrambled for a moment, as if his hooves were trying to find purchase on something slippery.

Then he climbed into the air, following the curve of the rainbow.

His mother met him at the edge of the cloud. She sniffed Dewdrop, then snorted as if to say, *Don't you go running off like that again.*

Then Cloud and Dewdrop turned to join the rest of the herd.

Lainey felt as if her heart were being squeezed. Joy and sadness were all mixed together—just like the sun and the rain. "Bye, little Dewdrop. I won't forget you," she whispered.

Although he couldn't have heard, Dewdrop stopped and looked back at her.

She had the feeling he was saying good-bye, too.

"She didn't even see me," Kate whispered.

Lainey glanced over at her friend. Kate was still staring after Cloud. Her face looked stricken. "She didn't recognize me at all."

Lainey opened her mouth, then closed it. What could she say? Nothing had gone the way they'd hoped. They hadn't found Fawn. They hadn't ridden back to Never Land to get more fairy dust. They'd returned Dewdrop to his family—that was all.

*At least it's something*, Lainey thought. Fawn, wherever she was, would be proud.

A scream sounded above them.

Lainey looked up to see a hawk barreling down from the sky. Its wings were spread wide, and its claws were extended.

The girls shrieked and ducked. The fairies scattered.

The hawk soared down and landed right in their midst. Lainey spied a familiar figure sitting on its back. "Fawn!" she cried.

# chapter 10

Fawn leaped off the goshawk's back. She fluttered joyfully between her friends. She pinched the girls' cheeks and hugged the other fairies.

"We didn't know how to find you. I thought you'd be with the mist horses," Lainey tried to explain. "But then you weren't—and we were so worried."

"Worried about me? Now, why would you do that?" Fawn winked. Her freckled face looked radiant.

Not just her face. Lainey realized that *all* of Fawn was aglow. "Wait a second. Fawn, you're glowing! And you can fly!" Fawn was flitting through the air like a lark, as if she'd never lost her magic.

What was going on? Had the miracle Lainey hoped for somehow come true?

"It's a very long story," Fawn said. "And I can't wait to tell it. But we've flown all over looking for you. The important thing now is that we get down this mountain."

The thought of walking back down the mountain, through the frightening forest, made Lainey's legs go weak. She sat down abruptly. "I don't think I can."

"Me either," said Mia. The other girls and fairies shook their heads. They were too tired from their long journey.

"Silly me. I almost forgot. I brought you something." Fawn flew over to the hawk. For the first time, Lainey noticed a miniature wooden barrel balanced between its wings. Fawn lifted it down easily. She placed it on the ground between Silvermist, Iridessa, and Rosetta.

"Go on." Fawn said, her eyes twinkling. "Open it."

Iridessa pried off the lid and gasped. "Fairy dust!"

The girls and fairies crowded around to see. The sparkling dust filled the barrel to the brim. When the light caught it, it shimmered with the colors of the rainbow.

"I don't understand," Iridessa said. "Where did you get this? Fairy dust only comes from—"

"Pixie Hollow." Fawn nodded. "You might say it was a gift from our friend Tink."

The girls and fairies gasped.

"Tinker Bell!"

"You found her!"

"Where is she?"

Everyone looked around, as if Tink might suddenly appear.

Fawn shook her head. "I haven't seen Tink. But I found her boat. The cargo hold is full of fairy dust. I know she won't mind if we borrow some." Fawn leaned forward. "I wanted to wait for Tink, but I knew it was more important to get the fairy dust to all of you. But if we go back to the boat, we might find her there!"

"Let's hurry," Iridessa said.

The fairies helped each other with the fairy dust, using their hands to sprinkle it over one another. As the dust settled over them, the fairies began to glow a bright lemon-yellow.

"I can fly again!" Rosetta rose into the air and flew a loop the loop.

Then it was the girls' turn. When Mia sprinkled a pinch of fairy dust over Lainey, her feet started to rise off the ground. She couldn't wait to fly!

They had just floated into the air when she heard a whinny.

A silver mare was galloping toward them across the sky. Her foal ran along beside her, lifting his knees high.

Kate's face lit up. "It's Cloud and Dewdrop! They came back!"

"How can they?" Mia asked.

"The wind died down," Lainey realized. "Look, they're coming to us!"

Cloud cantered right up to the ledge where Kate was standing. The great silver horse raised her nose. She snorted at Kate, as if to say, *Is that really you?*

"Oh, Cloud!" Kate threw her arms around the mare's neck. She buried her face in Cloud's mane. "You didn't forget me, after all."

Dewdrop danced around them, his little tail raised high. *See who I brought?* he seemed to be saying. *Didn't I do good?*

Lainey watched them with a lump in her throat. This time she wasn't jealous. She saw that she'd been wrong about her friend. Kate wasn't being bossy or showing off. She was only happy to see Cloud.

Kate lifted her head and whispered something in Cloud's ear. Then, with a move she must have practiced a hundred times in her dreams, Kate grabbed hold of

Cloud's mane and swung herself onto the horse's back.

Sitting astride Cloud, Kate smiled at her friends. "If it's okay with you guys, I'm going to take another way down."

She held out her hand to Lainey. "Want to ride with me? I know you like mist horses, too."

Lainey grinned. She grasped her friend's hand. Kate pulled her up onto Cloud's back.

"Ready?" Kate said.

Lainey wrapped her arms around her friend's waist. "Ready!"

Kate leaned forward. "Let's go, Cloud!"

Riding a mist horse was nothing like Lainey had imagined—it was better. Cloud was strong as thunder, graceful as the wind. As she galloped down the sky,

with Dewdrop running after her, Kate and Lainey whooped with joy.

All too soon, the ride was over. Cloud landed next to the waterfall and the pool where they had waded earlier that day.

Kate said good-bye to Cloud, squeezing her tight again. Lainey stroked Dewdrop's fuzzy mane one last time. "Be good," she told the little horse. "Don't run away from your mama."

Dewdrop nickered and nuzzled her hand.

They watched the horses take to the air, climbing higher and higher until they were just two gray dots. Then they vanished into the bright blue sky.

Kate and Lainey's friends soon joined them by the pool.

"When you think about it," Fawn was saying as she flew up, "if I hadn't lost my magic, I wouldn't have been carried away by the mist horses. And if they hadn't dropped me on the mountain, Striker never would have caught me. And if he hadn't caught me, I wouldn't have found Tinker Bell's boat. And if I hadn't found Tink's boat, I never would have found the fairy dust we needed." Fawn spread her arms. "In a way, losing my magic was the best thing that could have happened."

Rosetta made a face. "I don't know if I'd go that far. But I'm glad to be able to do this again."

She reached over and touched a drooping flower, making it bloom.

"And *I'm* glad to be able to do this again."

Silvermist scooped up a drop of water from the pool. She tossed it back and forth in her hands like a snowball.

"You wouldn't dare!" Rosetta grinned and ducked as Silvermist threw the ball of water at her.

Fawn frowned, watching them.

Usually, she liked to play. But now she felt edgy and impatient. She wanted to get to the boat to see if Tink had returned or at least left behind another clue.

"Come on," she told her friends. "The boat is this way."

Fawn led the fairies behind the waterfall. Lainey, Kate, Mia, and Gabby waited on the other side—the cave was too small for them to enter.

Inside the cave, Fawn looked around.

She was sure this was the right place. It was the same waterfall, the same dark cavern. But one thing was missing.

Tinker Bell's boat was gone.

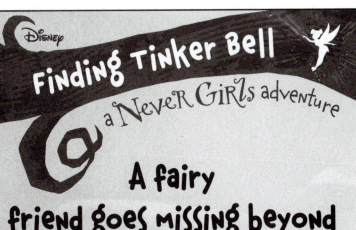

# Finding Tinker Bell

## a Never Girls adventure

A fairy friend goes missing beyond the Shores of Never Land . . .

Join the girls for all of their
Finding Tinker Bell adventures!

rhcbooks.com